AT THE SHOPS

Nicolas Brasch

NELSON
CENGAGE Learning

Australia • Brazil • Japan • Korea • Mexico • Singapore • Spain • United Kingdom • United States

NELSON
CENGAGE Learning

At the Shops

Fast Forward
Yellow Level 6

Text: Nicolas Brasch
Illustrations: Kim Fleming
Editor: Kate McGough
Series design: James Lowe
Design: Vonda Pestana
Production controller: Hanako Smith
Photo Research: Michelle Cottrill
Audio recordings: Juliet Hill, Picture Start
Spoken by: Matthew King and Abbe Holmes
Reprint: Siew Han Ong

Acknowledgements
The author and publisher would like to acknowledge permission to reproduce material from the following sources: Photographs by Fairfax Photos/Anthony Johnson, p7 top/Brenda Esposito, p5 centre/Craig Abraham, p8 top/Quentin Jones, p9 bottom left; Getty Images/AFP, pp 12 bottom, 14 bottom/Mario Tama, p14 top/Spencer Platt, pp 3, 5 bottom/Taxi, front cover, p1/Tim Boyle, p11 bottom; istockphoto.com, p6 bottom; Newspix/Annette Dew, p11 centre/Brianne Makin, p9 top/Gary Graham, p14 centre/Katrina Tepper, p10/Lindsay Moller, p7 centre/Sarah Rhodes, p11 top; photolibrary.com/AGE Fotostock/James Lauritz, p12 top/Burke Triolo Productions, p6 top/Doug Mazell, p9 bottom right; Reuters/Jason Reed, p15; Stock Photos/Lance Nelson, p8 bottom/Masterfile/George Simhoni, p4/Michael Mahovlich, p5 top/Zefa Images, pp 8 bottom, 6 centre, 13.

Text © 2007 Cengage Learning Australia Pty Limited

ISBN 978 0 17 012495 9
ISBN 978 0 17 012489 8 (set)

Cengage Learning Australia
Level 7, 80 Dorcas Street
South Melbourne, Victoria Australia 3205
Phone: 1300 790 853

Cengage Learning New Zealand
Unit 4B Rosedale Office Park
331 Rosedale Road, Albany, North Shore NZ 0632
Phone: 0508 635 766

For learning solutions, visit cengage.com.au

Printed in China by 1010 Printing International Ltd
10 15

THE UNIVERSITY OF
MELBOURNE

Evaluated in independent research by staff from the Department of Language, Literacy and Arts Education at the University of Melbourne.

AT THE SHOPS

Nicolas Brasch

Contents

Why We Have Shops

People buy things at shops.

People need shops because they cannot make or grow all the things they need.

People can shop day and night.

Some shops sell food.

Some shops sell clothes.

And some shops sell toys.

Shops That Sell Food

A lot of shops sell food.

Some food shops sell fruit.

Some food shops sell meat.

And some food shops sell fish.

These people work
in a fruit shop.
They are called **greengrocers**.

These people work
in a meat shop.
They are called **butchers**.

This man works in a fish shop.
He is called a **fishmonger**.

Some of the food sold in shops comes from farms.
Some of the food sold in shops comes from the sea.

Running Words 115

Food from farms and the sea
goes to the market.
People who have food shops
go to the market.
They buy food that goes
into the shops.
Then people come to the shops
and buy food.

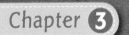

Chapter 3

Shops That Sell Clothes

A lot of shops sell clothes.

Some shops sell clothes
for boys and girls.

Some shops sell clothes for women.

Some shops sell clothes for men.

Some shops sell clothes for boys, girls, women and men!

Clothes that are sold in shops are not made in the shops.

Some clothes are made from things that grow on farms, like **cotton**.

The cotton from farms goes to a **factory**.
A factory is where things are made.
Clothes are made in factories.

From the factory,
the clothes go
to the shop.

Then people come
to the shop
and buy the clothes.

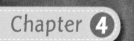

Chapter 4

Shops That Sell Toys

This is a toy shop.
The toys that are sold in this shop
are not made here.

Some toys are
made by people.

Some toys are made
in a factory.

14

When the toys are made, they go to the shop. Then people come to the shop and buy the toys.

Glossary

butchers   people who sell meat

cotton   a natural fibre that comes from a plant

factory   a place where goods are made, such as clothes or toys

fishmonger   a person who sells fish and other seafood

greengrocers   people who sell fruit and vegetables

Index